# NONNA'S STORIES - I

---

## FIRST OF THE SERIES

## TERESA DI SCLAFANI DE NASCA

# CONTENTS

**Nonna's Stories - I**

First in the series

Published by TecnoTur Publishing

Layout by Allan Tépper

ISBN of the paperback version:

979-8-9925106-7-6

ISBN of the electronic version (*ebook*):

979-8-9925106-8-3

# DEDICATION

*I dedicate this work to:*

*- My son, Professor Carlos Sayas Torres, who was born of a miracle. A hug and kiss from your mother who loves you so much.*

*- My sons Toni and Enzo.*

*- My three grandchildren, Salvatore Jesús, Enzito and Salvatore Antonio. Kisses to all.*

# EDITOR'S NOTE
## ABOUT THE WORD «NONNA»


The Italian word *Nonna* in English means Grandmother.

# 1

# HISTORY OF ALIA: GARDEN CITY

Alia is my village, where I was born on February 16, 1940 and my husband Salvatore Nazca on March 15, 1931. Our marriage was on August 22, 1959 and we left for Venezuela on November 22, 1959. I remember my childhood in a town blessed by God. It is on a mountain with a section below. The mountain is called *Pizzo della Raciura* and another ascent with stairs that leads to Rabatello, where the Calvary is located. During Holy Week the processions go by. There are prayers and songs before, there is the Mother Church next to the palace Guccione where on July 2 the biggest feast of the year is celebrated, the Madonna, where all the apostles, the virgins, St. Joseph and the Sorrowful are. There is a clock that at 4 o'clock in the morning wakes the people up. There is the San José Church, which is very small, and the Santa Ana Church, which is large and full of memories. On the staircase there are bars, a souvenir left by Salvatore Nazca when he was 16 years old.

That town of Alia was saved from being destroyed, because they realized that the cannons were too low and put them high. The Lopresti family, an heiress of Alia, wealthy landowners of whom I am an heir through my dad's and mom's two grandmothers, always had a party. One flaw was that the employees were not given anything. That's how the revenge was: One icy morning they left all the cattle outside and only the bull was saved and went to the *grotto*, that's why it's called the Tabaro Grotto, which is near the gate.

There were two schools: one in San José, very old, for young people and geniuses, and the new school for boys. There were several very good teachers. There was the teacher Macaluso, with whom everyone was frightened because he was very demanding. One day a week he would take them to the fields to work on his land.

The sea is 30 km away and the first time I saw it I was 8 years old. My dad and I were going to Palermo to visit Dr. Gucciones and I remember that from the top of the train my dad told me: «See the sea.» My father took him faba beans, since it was the season When we arrived, my sister-in-law was very happy and shouted. The pasta with *fritella*. On Monday they took me for an X-ray. At that time, it was like a long and high closet and there was a bar that passed through them to make them. The result was the same as today.

It was the time of Benito Mussolini's fascism, who was the «dog» of the monarchy and threw out the monarch Philip II, sent him into exile and took over. Those were very bad times, Italy was backward, without water, electricity or plumbing.

Behind the house, there was a street where my dad used to throw garbage and he put a pipe to the bridge. Everything went under the bridge. It was about 200 m away and it was the National Road. And that's how we lasted until the fall of Mussolini. They deny it, but it's true that he gave the poor 10 g of bread per day and 100 g of meat per week to the family.

Those who had land and cattle lived well. My grandfather Gaetano Di Sclafani sailed to New York in 1906 on a ship full of Sicilians. We have the picture of all the surnames that traveled with him. The dollar was US dollar was valuable and in Italy it was the lire. With only 2 years that he was there, he bought land, house and cattle. We lived well, we were middle class.

Sicily was invaded by the Spaniards and French and there were the Sicilian Vespers, in which men, women and children came out. After 5 o'clock in the afternoon the word was *ciciri*. If they did not know how to pronounce it, outside they said, they were thrown out.

Alia is at the bottom of a mountain of «ovaries«. We climbed up to the *Pizzo della Raciura* and it was easier on the way up than the way down. There was the feast of *Natal (birth)*on the 31st of the year, where there were parties. Sweets were made and we got the new dress at the curtain place with windows. There were weets and two coals in the sleeves of the dress. That was a family party. Carnival came in February, the last days were the shepherd's feast. There was dancing and lots of food. There was the Calvary where people went during Holy Week to pray and sing. There is a rural area called Marcatobianco. My dad had the land nearby and with the neighbors he would go to the feast of the crucifix in the month of May.

There were horse races, lots of food, vendors of everything. People took advantage of the opportunity to buy. Every Sunday, Father Cuchiara would give mass. There was only one teacher who taught all of the grades. They were all very rich, all landowners with a lot of land and cattle that belonged to Castronovo. Life in the village was good for us because we had land and cattle we lived very well. Dad used to go to the fair to sell cattle. He used to wear pants with black leather on the knee, summer pants and a hat. That's the memory I have, the laying hens. I remember that the chickens would come home alone. If a pig grew and was killed in October, sausages, lard and butter were made. In spite of everything, life was very good, because the people who worked had enough to eat every day.

2

# TALKING ABOUT MIRACLES

A 32-year-old woman became pregnant. She worked a lot with transportation and her own vehicle. When she lacked vehicles, she called the Colombian cooperatives on the border. Those were serious times and the work did not give much profit. Her husband worked from Puerto la Cruz to La Vergareña, near Brazil. She got pregnant in 1972 and went to the pharmacy nearby. They gave her two pills and she miscarried a fetus the size of a hand. Frightened, she called a neighbor and told her: «That fetus was a boy».

She went to Puerto Rico and a child was born. This lady had two apparitions of a young man about 25 years old. She came from Orlando. She had a son with a business. She was very tired when she arrived at the airport in Caracas and a young man appeared to her and said: «Lie down». She told him: «I am afraid, there are thieves». He had a backpack and took off her books and put it under her head. Then he took off his hat and put it on top of her. «I'll wake you up,» he tells her. They call her at 8 o'clock because the plane was about to leave. He tells her, «Mommy, Mommy, your plane is leaving.» She gets up and says, «My guardian angel, when will I see you?» and he responds, «I don't know.»

Another time at the same airport, the young men started to say that rats were coming out at dawn. One of the young men went to look for an armchair or a chair, and said to her: «Lie down, we are going to take care of the rats.» When the plane was about to leave, they called her. The things of life. This young man comes to the United States after a long time, graduated in Puerto Rico as a surgeon cardiologist. He was an eminent surgeon and came to the United States about 6 years ago.

At the hospital a lady said to her son «Find me a cardiologist». She saw on the Internet that there was an outstanding one, made an appointment and went there. She says she liked him. He then moved to a closer hospital and made very consistent appointments. Once, looking him in the eye, he said «A wooden picture with a carved frame that says professor such-and-such». I don't want to put his first name, let alone his last name, he is well known. He continued his sympathy between the two of them.

A very Catholic old man says to this lady: «I am very religious and I study reincarnation a lot. You should have your DNA done». She had it done. On May 20, she went for a consultation and on May 28, he told her that this lady had been given a new life. All her family is in Italy and she always goes to Mother Church and talks with Monsignor, who is 93 years old. He replied: «Miracles do exist». That was an incarnation, like the Virgin Mary who the Angel Gabriel announced to her that she was going to be a mother. The resemblance is that he gave her intelligence, kindness, hardworking, humility, everything is coinciding with the demeanor of the lady.

She arrives in the United States and inquired with a very old Father and he tells her the same thing. She tells him to go to the Bishop, but he is too busy and cannot. She made him a well worded letter. She transcribed it to the Pope and is waiting for a reply.

# 3

# HOMEMADE PASTA

In the village, pasta was made at home with an *abridio*, with a hole in the stove and a bar that was turned. The pasta came out, all kinds you wanted. The grain went to grind far away where there were the mafias and sometimes they took it away. The bread was made in the machine and a wooden oven.

During Holy Week, we made the *martorio* in front of Santa Ana Church. The Church rented the chairs in San José on March 19 and made sweet bread and canolas filled with ricotta cheese. Virgin figures were made for the poor, the virgins of St. Joseph and other 12. A very big table was made and all those who belonged to St. Joseph and the Immaculate Virgin attended. They attended the washing of the feet during Holy Week.

For the young people during Holy Week, there were exercises in the Church at dawn and the girls would throw cakes at them. Some girls who had boyfriends would take a small piece of clothing and go with the boyfriend, stay out for a few days and return beating their breasts, so that their parents would forgive them.

**4**

## ITALY AND THE WARS

Great sacrifices had to be made to get ahead and after the war of 1518, Italy was destroyed and starved, with people on foot and many dead. In the Second World War it was also destroyed and only the Vatican was spared. Pope Pius V went out to meet the soldiers to ask them not to enter the Vatican and was saved, history says.

The Germans never paid the pending damages for the many dead and many maimed, many widows and orphans. At that time, the Italian government gave a pittance of pensions, because it had no money. Those were times of terror. The Americans sent used clothes, powdered milk and chickpea flour to make *polenta*.

Venezuela in the time of emigration was a country that received many Italian, Portuguese, islanders, Spaniards and immigrants from all other countries that wanted to emigrate.

Those were rich, happy times, times of Juan Vicente Gómez, Angarita and General Pérez Jiménez. The latter was thrown out on January 23, 1958 and Venezuela became worse, being a land rich in oil and all minerals.

Then the Adecos, President Betancourt and Leoni arrived, as well as Copei and Caldera. Carlos Andres came and mortgaged the country. Luis Herrera did not steal, but he made the others steal. Caldera again, the Chávez dictatorship and most recently, the Maduro dictatorship.

More than 7 million Venezuelans have left to seek their luck in other countries. They were ruined and everything was stolen. Now a democratic wins and they do not give him the job. They keep sneaking out, looking for other horizons. They end up like the Cubans here in the United States, a very rich country that is almost like the third world.

Hopefully, a good government will come so that we can live in peace. All Latin America is not well, people abandoned the countryside and believe that in other countries they will live better. They do not know that the countryside is what produces.

Italians have gone around the world, working in every field, lifting up countries that were in bad shape. Italy has not been lucky either with its governments. If it were not for tourism, which attracts more than 30 million people a year, it would not be possible to survive. Restaurants are inexpensive, hotels exist with a range of prices, even family houses. That's why tourists go there, because it's economical. There is a subway that goes all over Europe. There are many beautiful churches and in France the best church in the world.

Italy has beautiful churches and good squares. That's why tourists go to Turin, where the shroud of the Magdalene is located, with which she wiped the sweat of God. In Padua is the living tongue of St. Anthony. There is the Strait of Messina, where you have bus and trolley. You can eat the *arancinis* in Palermo and there are the squares of Montello, which are the best in the world.

Then there is the Murriales Church, the Tower of Pisa that sinks from one side, little by little. There are many souvenirs from England, the old things in front of the Tower of Pisa, the church that is 18 karat gold.

England is a monarchy and where today there is no life, after Queen Elizabeth died. It is possible that it will change with the new King and with the grandchildren. The King of Spain has changed many rules and his salary is a small sum. There are several islands that have very modern kingdoms. There are many beautiful stories and memories.

# 5

## GIULIANO

There are writers who say that Giuliano was always a bandit and that he was beheaded. It is not true: He became a bandit because of necessity and circumstances. The police were in league with the Mafia. Mafiosos passed by with vehicles full of weapons and drugs and they made them pass. Instead Giuliano passed by on a bicycle with some sacks of flour and they took them away from him. He armed himself with a crowbar and killed two policemen. He went underground, taking from the rich and giving it to the poor. He would go into houses and people would let him. I remember very well. Unfortunately, his cousin betrayed him and he was killed.

The war in Trieste left many dead as in Italy. There were soldiers who stayed in Trieste and married and there were those who returned. A soldier fell in love with Dona Lola, an only daughter of a rich family, and took her to Sicily deceiving her, saying that he was rich. Of all the mansions he showed her, he said that his was the best, until he arrived in the village of Alia in a neighborhood of Santa Rosalia where her parents lived.

The woman saw that it was a poor neighborhood. First, she was very much in love and second, her father told her that if she left, she should not return. The woman got used to that shack and the need in which she lived. She never complained. She was satisfied with everything. She had brought luxury clothes and her paintings. If she went to fill the water downstream from where she lived, I remember that she was criticized for her fancy clothes and her paintings. Even when we left school we would shout: «Lady Lola with three canola, one dances for you, and two sing for you».

It is unfortunate. She wrote a book of her life that was successful after she died and another she wrote about the life of the people of Alia. She also wrote lies about people, wore studded shoes and lies. My grandmother was from 1890 and died in 1972. She wore shoes with little heels, purse and jacket. Sister Ana always wore a hat and they say she wore a veil like the Muslims. I subscribed to the trustee to withdraw all those lying books. People today know that it is a lie, but in 20 years, the youth will not know that it is a lie.

6

# THE MAFIA AND THE COUNTRYSIDE

For many years the military, governments and courts were all Mafia. They killed, threatened, demanded money. The poor were killed because they had none, the rich were charged «vaccines». There were other Mafias that demanded gold things, night tables, lamps, dressing tables, even chairs. The thievery was too much. There were pianos and musical instruments and they organized parties where everyone went. Very rich people who enjoyed themselves at the expense of the workers, they took their blood by working in the fields.

Before, whoever worked the land was given half and had to provide the seeds and chemicals, and they had nothing left. Later, with the agrarian reforms, the seeds and chemicals were given to the owner. The peasants had to take the ears off of corn. There were round areas where they put the ears of corn and with two mules they began to trample all those ears. Since they wore a headscarf, they were called the Virgins of Gibilmanna.

They took out the body and soul until they could divide the grain with the straw. The grain was taken for sale and the straw was piled up for food in the winter, for the animals and cattle. Some people used to have a feast in the village. They would give them wine to drink and they would give them grain, in the feast of the Madonna Santa Rosalia la Dolorosa. They had parties with music and singers and everyone put their goods up for sale. They don't make those parties anymore, since times are complicated with a lot of costs.

There were many who acted on behalf of the Mafias and those were worse. They didn't know what they were doing but the strong ended up with them. They were the bad deaths. There were counter-mafias, big groups that some-times ended badly if they didn't hang on.

That was a very bad time, children were stolen to cross borders and others were stolen for ransom. There was a hospital where nuns and a priest made newborns disappear and sold them to blacks, who paid a high price for them. That happened a lot in Argentina. When these children were grown up, they saw that they were white and their parents were black, they began to suspect that they were not their children and they searched everywhere until they found out who the parents were.

Today many have returned. There are singles. There are fathers who return with their wives and children. There are those who find their mothers alive and there are those who are already dead. In Argentina, families still go to the Plaza Primero de Mayo (First of May Square) crying for their children. It is lamentable the atrocity that a mother went through for another who sold herself for a fistful of money. Sad story. People die; stories remain. The history of a piece of country is very long and complicated.

7

# BAKING BREAD

First you have to prepare the land to pass a specific plow and then remove all the bush. In April, the seeds have to be sown and the seeds have to be chemically treated in order to grow. In the month of June, men and women separate the ears with the trunk, the ears in the air, the trunk is bound with the same straw. They make large areas and clean them to put the ears and start the treading. Men and women, the husband treading with two mules and the women taking the ears out of the area that was coming out and throwing them inside. They set aside the straw and the grain that was going to be sold, because it was necessary to leave to eat during the year.

When they went to the mill to grind, it was necessary to remove all the debris and small stones and take them to the mill. The flour from kneading the bread in a wooden mesh, adding yeast and water and kneading it. The oven is heated with wood, very hot, first on one side and then on the other side. Remove the ash, put the round bread in it and keep it for about half an hour. Take it out and put it in a basket ready to eat. The people who eat it do not see the work that gets bread on the table.

There are stories of firewood to make bread. You put a very small seed, if it is from the mountains it is better. You have to pour water every day or it dries up. Look for water from a river, sometimes near and sometimes far away, wait for them to get big, which will take years. Remove the branches that were used for cooking and stoves. The trunk is removed, cut into small pieces and heated in the oven with them. To cook the bread, coals are made that are used for the stoves. Today, young people don't know how much work a piece of bread used to cost. There is an electric oven and hot bread every day. Nice stories.

8

# THE TALE OF THE LITTLE RED LINTY

The little redhead wore a hairpin on her head and lived with her parents and siblings. Her grandparents lived far away but they went every day, because they loved her grandmother and grandfather very much. One day, she said to his mother: «I'm going to go to my grandparents». Her mother said: «Be very careful». She replied, «Don't worry, Mom, I know how to take care of myself. »

She set out on the road to his grandparents, crossing mountains, trees and many dangers, but the most dangerous thing was still coming. She meets a parrot and says: «Where are you going, Little Red Linty?». «To my grandparents.» She walks, finds a pigeon and says: «Where are you going, Little Red Linty?» She says: «To my grandparents». She keeps on walking and finds a little bird: «Where are you going, little red head?» «To my grandparents» and she goes on. She finds a kitten who says: «Where are you going, redhead?» «To my grandparents.» She keeps walking. «Where are you going, little red fluffy?» says a little sheep. «To my grandparents.» She keeps walking. «Where are you going, little redhead?» says the wolf. «I'm going to my grandparents.» «I'm going to eat you,» and he opens his big mouth.

She starts to run scared and a man passes by with his wife. He grabs her and puts her in his wife's arms. She struggles not to do anything to her, pulls out a knife and kills the wolf. The Little Red Linty tells him: «I beat you, wolf. You're dead and I'm alive and I'm going to my grandparents. You stay dead and we're going to burn you».

# 9

## MY BROKEN WRIST

There was a little girl whose father bought her a doll. In wartime nobody had dolls and she played every day with her little friends. The little girl was very pretty and charming. There was a parking next door to Aunt Concetta's house and two nephews who had a carpentry shop. One of the nephews was Giuseppe, tall and handsome, and the other was Ciccito, short and cheerful.

The children came every day to see what furniture was available for them. Giuseppe was serious and didn't look at them, but Ciccito was playful and played with them. They had to give him hugs and kisses and he made their cribs, tables and two little chairs. Until one day there was a cat and he took it out of her hands and broke it. The little girl cried a lot.

## 10

# THE END OF THE WAR

Many returned badly wounded, others without clothes and shoes, skinny but happy because they had accomplished their objectives: to win the war for the homeland with the help of the U.S. military.

Italy was destroyed and without money, pure waste. The green trucks were in every town, throwing candies and chocolates, bringing joy to the children. They went to Palermo, the best city in Sicily. Palermo, «The Golden Conch».

They danced, played the best music and played soccer with the children. What a joy! Moments of happiness. They bathed in Montello's best beach. People brought them food and drink: a real party.

Italy was going to think about reconstruction. The Italians fixed it and little by little, the reconstruction began. There was a lot of garbage left by the Germans, who did not bother to collect all the weapons they left behind. At last a clean and disease-free Italy. «Long live Italy!» shouted the military and the people accompanied them with enthusiasm, because Italians do not want wars.

11

## VENEZUELA

A country rich in oil, gold, diamonds, bauxite, minerals and all the riches that God could give.

Emigration was very large, from all countries of the world. There were Indians and indigenous mixed with blacks. Someone fell because of the loneliness they had with those very bad people. People felt lonely. There were those who took their families with them and there were those whose families did not want to go. Those people had a hard time. The Maracuchas (women from Maracaibo) went crazy for an Italian or other nationalities.

I knew of several cases and I will mention two very serious ones. One died and it is not known if he was killed. He had sent some savings and two months later the news of his death arrived. The widow, his old mother, three females and a small boy, who had to work since they were very young, were left behind.

Another lady from Spain was ready to travel with her children, a boy and a girl. She got the news that a woman had killed him because she found out that his wife was arriving with the children and killed him out of jealousy. The lady was ready to travel, so she traveled and got a job in a school and then she worked in insurance. She worked very hard to support the family.

She married a barber and the children studied. The male had an educational career and the female the same. The male became a school principal, a great gentleman. That was the emigration. There are those who won and those who lost. This is the sad story.

12

# DON QUIXOTE OF LA MANCHA

The knight-errant of modern life. The youth must know this history from their life experiences, with historical and intellectual training. They were heroes of the time, medical specialists, heroes of literature.

In 1605, the publications of Miguel de Cervantes faced several situations. His life was the literature and different from that time, the literature of the archpriest for the celestinas with folkloric backgrounds that were handled at that time. Don Quixote and Sancho are not the same character, nor the same style. Even with the literature itself, Miguel de Cervantes is confronted with people who are frowned upon.

Other resources were addressed and there was no point of reference. You had to study the creations of Don Quixote to read his original writings. It does not look like a novel, it is very curious and picturesque, dressed in very colorful clothes. You have to read his stories, with their ideologies distant from the modern world. The tales of *The Thousand and One Nights*, where he dreamed a thousand nights and did not conclude his dreams. Adventures that could be seen as the war of the century.

Cervantes was born in the city of Trento, which was inaugurated before he was born and closed when he was 15 years old. Ludovico came to Spain and his cannons were not yet there. It was the time of Emperor Charles V, the Jesus Campaign and Christian thought. There was the Battle of Lepanto in past centuries under the command of Don John of Austria, who returned from captivity, absent from the homeland.

Luis remains in captivity while Cervantes was in Africa, with more hatred and power, with false deceptions. He can say «Here is my homeland». Luis was in the prison of the Inquisition and Cervantes was in the prison of Africa. As much as there is hatred and deceit, bitter, the soldiers of Lepanto are defeated and full of many projects. The invincible armada that triumphs, the pirate, is that there is jubilation. The new defeat is confirmed and the future is thought of. Cervantes' experience was decisive. It closed the life of 40 years.

The heroics of Lepanto begin with Don Quixote, the knight, and more than armed with iron, he only raises his strength blindly. He is superhuman. Defeated with great faith and reason, like the ships that Philip II had sent to fight the storms. After the storm comes the calm. The wind, the sky, says Cervantes, is the heroic attitude of Don Quixote.

The court of death, the wedding feast of Camacho, the caves of Montesino, the adventures, the mockery of the things of the Dukes. Don Quixote enters the city and attends the ladies' party, being forced to dance with them.

In 1569, Cervantes was in Rome, a fugitive from Spain because of his wounds. Antonio de Sigura condemns him to rebellion, in the service of Giulio Acquaviva who was Cardinal in 1570. Soon he will sit in soldier's places, in the company of Captain Diego de Urbina, Miguel de Moncada's cousin who embarked on La Marquesa.

On October 7, 1571, the Christian armada was commanded by John of Austria. Eight years later the Turkish navy was recognized in the naval battle. Miguel de Cervantes was ill and upset. The captain and his friends told him that he was sick, that he should stay in bed. He replied that no, he would stay fighting for God and the King. They told him not to go on deck because of his illness. He fought with the Turks as a soldier.

Juan de Austria tried to finish the naval battle and was wounded in one hand, the left, which was left with a defect. Cervantes was cured and returned as a soldier participating in several military actions.

In 1780, the Royal Spanish Academy wanted to recover the most reliable text. John Baule, pastor of the Church of Edmonton, published in 1781 in London and Salzburg accompanied by several writings.

Cervantes, language and knowledge, the modern study will reach a character. The Brussels edition of 1607, the Madrid edition of 1636 and 1637, were independent of each other with graphic and romantic requirements. The squires have to leave the banquet and their souls are darkened by not being able to eat at the banquet, the important meal. Camacho's feast is in the 1605 editions and in Madrid in 1765.

To do justice, says the author, to keep there. Cervantes is playing with the expression to keep fasting and to keep the feasts, to observe the precepts of the church. El clever Hidalgo Don Quijote de la Mancha, composed by Miguel de Cervantes Saavedra, directed by the Marquis Gibraleón, Count of Benalcázar y Bañares, Viscount of the Puebla de Alcocer, Lord of the Villas of Capilla, Curiel and Burguillos, with privileges in Madrid by Juan de la Cuesta.

They begin the old turns, Kings VII 1254 in the modern ones and Samuel VII 1254. The stories name the river Mole. It was said by the King of Spain with birth at home and death at sea. Oceans kissing the walls of the famous city of Lisbon. In the opinion of the golden sands, it is about thieves who tell the stories of cacos, those of choirs, the harlot women with the bishops of Mondoñedo, who will lend Lamia, Laida and Flora who have credits of cruelty.

Princess Dulcinea, mistress of the captive heart and many grievances. I'm going to say goodbye, do not reproach me for the rigor of the afflictions and beauty in her heart that lacks love. I see Don Quixote fallen and in love, humiliated of the fortress.

What did you think of the sales? For me, gentleman from Castile, for me anything is good. My thing is weapons, my rest is to fight as a soldier. I am never a knight of well-served ladies, as Don Quixote was, when he came from his village with some maidens who cured him. His precious princess. Rocinante the name, my lady, of my horse, and Don Quixote of La Mancha, my post, who would not like to discover me for the deeds done in your service.

Romance from old men from Sasporote, replies Don Quixote, because I understand, it hurts my case. He comes from that day to the ribs, he calls haddock, Andalusia, cod. God make your mercy very fortunate, knight, and give him good fortune. What happened to the knight when he went out to the inn at dawn, dashing and boisterous? The armed gentleman with joy burst the saddle of the horse, coming to the memory to take with me the memories and the shirt for the office and the escudería.

Rocinante knows the querencias, the thanks I give to heaven, walking with feet on the ground. The farmer lowers his head and answers a word. Don Quixote asks him how much he owes him. 73 reales is the amount. Tell them that I will pay them at once. The villain replies in passing that he was sworn and that he swore to nothing more. I am going to receive three shoes that I gave him and the two stilts. I have no money here, come walk with me, let's pay the barber, Sancho is ill. What harm is the gentleman doing, I don't have any money. It's a bad year, Mr. Bartolomeo.

The disgrace of the knight, oh noble Marquis of Mantua, my uncle and lord carnal reigning and wife, with the love of the emperor's son. Lord Quijana I must call you when I have judgment. Sosegado with the gentlemen goes on with the romance. To all whom he asks, to Don Rodrigo de Narvaez and the Marquis of Mantua or Pedro Alonso, my neighbors, your worship is not Valdovino or Abindarráez, but the honored Hidalgo of Senor Quijana. «I know who I am,» replies Don Quixote, «and I know that I can speak with twelve French peers. »

Nicolás is the name of the barber, reading adventure books day and night. So goes Mr. Reinaldo Montalbán, the knight of the Cross, mirror of chivalry. The second outing of our knight Don Quixote de la Mancha, of the most valiant Don Quixote, was in the adventures of the windmills. There are already 23 that people say they like his adventures. The discreet reason, I spent with his master of the adventures, which passed with dead body and with new events.

I am a knight of La Mancha, called Don Quixote. If it does not satisfy you, love them easily, it will be your mercy the freedom that Don Quixote gave to many unfortunates. For the evil of his degrees he takes them where he will, staying with the barber to serve the soldiers. What happens to the famous Don Quixote? In Sierra Morena, which is one of the greatest adventures of this true knight, whose story will be told.

Either he lacks love or knowledge, he has too much cruelty or sorrows, who treats strangers. What is Sierra Morena? Let it happen to the brave knight of La Mancha and of the invitations who did penance. Beltenebros, sovereignty and high ladies, the icy absence has reached the heart of the sweetest Dulcinea del Toboso.

I send you the health that he does not have. Thou art beauty that scorns me, may thy courage for thy scorn and my affiancing woman, may I be chance suffered by thy heart. Hold me in your bed, brave companion, keep me lasting. My good squire Sancho will give thee whole relation, fair and ungrateful, beloved heart, my enemy. In the world of struggles and causes, see if you would like me, my beloved, if not, end my life. I will make sacrifices and you will always be cruel to my desires. Thus I go on until death.

The knight of the sad figure, trees, grasses and bushes that in this place are so tall and green. You are my evil, you are. Listen to my lament, you heal my pains. I do not abhor thee, love, though thou art terrible, thou art a bird. Don Quixote mourns the absence of Dulcinea del Toboso and here, the place where my beloved is, loyal to her lord hides and has come to many evil. Without knowing the heart, love is of bad thorn, so to the pipote.

Here Don Quixote mourns the absence of Dulcinea del Toboso, who wanders with her heart in search of adventures. By hard sorrows, cursing strangers and for with watering and with sorrows, he finds sad adventures. Love with scourge, with companion plants, begging the heart. Here Don Quixote mourns the absence of Dulcinea del Toboso.

Evil writings calmed with their intentions. The priest and the barber are something else, worthy of being told in this humble story that deals with new, pleasant and petty things. The priest and the barber shake even the saws they have, sister Dorotea discretions, another thing of tastes and pastimes. It was about crafty artifices, about orders. Enamored knight of hope, penances he did to be forgiven, the tasty food does not invite me.

Reasoning passing by the fountain, Don Quixote and Sancho Panza, is the nation's squire and impertinent soldier who saved the people. What happens? What happened to the people and reason? The gangs of Don Quixote until they tell the novels of the impertinent soldier. It increases the pain to the people and ends the impertinence, increases the shame to Don Pedro. For the day the saint prostrates himself there is no one. He is ashamed of himself, to see the sinner with his magnetism with breasts of shame. Not only to move him the lookout, how shameless. Oh, heart! He is moved to be a lookout who is ashamed to look that he is in heaven and earth.

The woman involved does not move, does not touch and is not seen, with her mask she wears so as not to look at the heart. It is better that she stands up and sanity is put on. There is danger of breaking, what hurts my heart is the opinion that are all with reason of points. That if there are Danaes in the world, there are showers of gold and that cries the heart. I seek death and life, opinion and freedom, the closed exits with the traitor. Loyal with death from which you never expect anything of good, with heaven and with its statutes, the impossible even more than where are the novels of the curious impertinent.

The silence of the nights when in the sweet sleep of mortals and the poor, count the impertinent rich who do not love people. When the sun goes away, it is lost by the rosy with the oriental sighs, with sighs and unequal accents. There are the old quarrels renewing the presents and when the sun is starry, making rays on the earth, the weeping grows and the moaning in the mortal encounter. The sky is deaf and has no ears. I die, it does not believe me. Moreover, I close my eyes to die and as it is true, I return to oblivion and you can see me.

To oblivions, lives and glories deserted, today they will put in the chest, dead as brothers. The face is carved in the desert. Today if you see my chest open, with beautiful face that is carved in the relics, with the hard trance threatens me and threatens me. May he give you strength who sails, who threatens and defies your own strength, he who sails with the dark sky by sea and sky, dangerous way where it is north and it is port. He must seek out huge battles, which Don Quixote awaits with leather and red wine, and with great success that sells and shakes him.

Where come the stories of the famous infanta Micomicona, with stars, graceful adventure that softens the heart. In this barren land, brought down these clods by the ground the holy soul of three thousand soldiers. They climbed with lively and better dwellings, being first in vain that they exert with force their strenuous stroke to the end. It is little, weary, has life at the edge of the swords. This is the beloved soil that softens the heart.

My memory is blind in the past centuries, present in the heart better prestige, wait for his hard breasts open the clear sky. Souls climbed to heaven, still he held bodies of brave seeking good people. What happened one day far away, the sale of other peoples, many worthy to know. Sweet is my hope, breaking the weeds that follow the firm way. Thou thyself straighten, faint to see thee at every step together, and of thy death shall not lazy reach, honest triumphs without victories. Some who may be blissful, those contrasting this and fortune come to deliver helpless leisure, soft with all the senses, love and its glory come with face to reason.

When you come there is no fair contract. There is no better pledge than that of the heart, carat to 800 for his tastes. And whoever shows no esteem for the few amorous beads that he or she cherishes, perhaps reaches the firmament, impossible to follow because it tempers the heart. Perhaps it reaches the sky with mine and of love one day, difficult the effect with so much voice that Don Quixote gave, opening from door to door the sales to surrender him the heart.

Where the inquiry is finished, where the godmothers of the albarda gave other adventures, but the whole truth happened. What will seem to your worship, madam, said the barber who affirmed this. Gentilhombre still porfía that is in the hall, Mr. Belmo that tried to convince the goatherd in all those who carried the brave Don Quixote, the academics of the organillos and of the overbearing soldier.

Life and death shake hands and valiant Don Quixote of La Mancha, the calvatrueno that adorned La Mancha, with spoils that pass from Crete the judgment of the sharp weather vanes, were better wide the arm of the forces. So much they widen that they arrive of the Cathay until Gaeta the most hideous and most discreet muses that engraved verses in bronze plates and that tails left the Amadises. It is very little, to Galaores had estribando in his love and bizarries, the one that made silence to the Belianises, the one that in Rocinante wandering wandered, lies under this cold slab.

This one you see, the face amondongado, high chest and also spirited, in Dulcinea queen of Toboso, of whom the great Quixote was fond. He trod for her one and the other side of the great Sierra Negra, and the famous soldier in Montiel's fields, to the beautiful plain of Aranjuez, on foot and tired because of Rocinante. Oh, hard star! And that manchega lady invited you andante knight, in tender years she left dying writings, could not hear of loves with anger and deceit, of capricious and discreet academics of the argamasillas, in praise of Rocinante, horse of Don Quixote of La Mancha.

Erratum: I saw this book entitled Segunda parte de Don Quijote de la Mancha composed by Miguel de Cervantes Saavedra and there is nothing in it worthy of note that does not correspond to its original. Dated in Madrid on October 21, 1615.

Approval by commission and mandates of the lords of the councils and made to see the book contained in this memorial, does not contain anything against faith or morals. The book of much lawful entertainment mixed with much moral philosophy may be given license to print it, in Madrid on November 5, 1615.

Approval and mandate of the Lords of the Council. I have seen the second part of Don Quixote de la Mancha by Miguel de Cervantes Saavedra, and it contains nothing against our holy Catholic faith or good morals, but much honest recreation and peaceful amusement that the ancients judged suitable for their republics. Even the stern of the Lacedaemonians erected statues and laughter, and those of Thessaly dedicated feasts to him, as Pausanias says, referred to by Bosius, books *De signis Ecclesiae*. Encouraging withered spirits and melancholy spirits.

Of what Tulio remembered, in the first *De legibus* and the poet, saying «*Interpone tuis interdum gaudia curis*», what the author does mixing the true bulls, the sweet and the profitable and the moral to the facets, dissimulating in the bait of the donaire, the hook of the reprehension of the books of chivalry. For with good diligence, the illustrious man of our nation has mostly cleansed the admiration and envy of strangers from his contagious honor. This is my opinion, except in Madrid on March 17, 1615.

Approval by commission, Mr. Gutiérrez de Cetinos, Vicar General of this Villa de Madrid, Court of His Majesty. I have seen the book of the second part, Ingenious gentleman Don Quixote de la Mancha, has the privilege on his part of Miguel de Cervantes Saavedra, was not made relatación that has composed the second part of Don Quixote de la Mancha, of which there is presentation by the book of stories. The Mayor of the Houses and Court, Chancery and any others, justice of all the city, villas and place of our kingdoms and lordships and each one in his jurisdiction to those who are now as they will be from now on. That he keeps and fulfills this our cell that we make against them, not to pass in any way penalties to our mercy of ten thousand maravedí for our chamber. Dated at Madrid, the 30th day of the month of May, 1615 years. I, the King. By mandate of the King, our lord Pedro de Contreras.

13

# THE STORY OF A FAMILY THAT DENIES THE RIGHT TO BE BORN

There was a rich and powerful family in 1753, consisting of father, mother and two daughters. The father was very powerful and arrogant and one of the daughters fell madly in love with a man who was not of her condition. The father, because of his arrogance, wanted nothing to do with this affair and did not want the daughter to have children. The girl disobeyed the father and had children, helped by her nanny.

The father gave orders to disappear the child and spoke to an obedient slave laborer. When the nanny fell asleep, he took the child and left him adrift. Immediately the nanny wakes up, realizes that the child is not there and how maddened she goes to the street. She runs into the man and they argue. The black woman promises him that they will never hear from her or the child.

She goes and finds the man who had the child and who had already put him in a bush, embraces him and takes him away. The master had given her some money to sustain her for the first few months. She walked until she got sores on her feet, arrived at a small ranch and went inside. She began to look for work in town, washing and ironing, and got it. It was a job she did when the child slept and so she began to buy him clothes and shoes.

The child was happy: the first steps, the school. Sometimes he had to spend a lot of money to buy shoes and he went to school with broken shoes. One day, another boy grabbed him, hit him hard and threw him in the mud, from where he got up well beaten. At that moment, a very elegant and nice man passes by and drops his wallet. The boy sees it and takes it.

The grateful man wanted to give him some money, but he refused, saying that Mama Dolores had not taught him to accept gifts. The grateful man asked him where he lived and he told him that he lived in a small shack. The gentleman went at night to visit them and the black woman was grateful for the visit of a rich man to a little shack. He tells them: «From today on all the expenses of this child are on my account, since he wants to study medicine». The black woman tells him: «I would like him to be a lawyer» but the boy insists on medicine. Years go by, the boy grows up and studies, always dressed elegantly.

Meanwhile, in the rich man's house there were parties. The daughters did not want to come down but he told them they had to come down or else he would beat them. One night the boy's benefactor, who was a friend of the father's, came. He asked one of the daughters to dance and after that night he would go to visit her. He fell in love with her, but she replied that she would not marry him or anyone else. One night she confided her secret to him. The man was moved and realized that it was the same boy and the same black woman.

The boy became a first class doctor, he passed with flying colors. As he became a famous doctor, all the rich people called him. One day the rich grandfather called him and he went there all the time. He was well received and was thought to be on a par with them. In the house lived the granddaughter who fell madly in love with him and he with her. He confided to her that he had no last name, but she replied that she did not care.

One day while the benefactor was visiting, the grandfather began to say that he was not in her good graces. The grand-daughter insisted that she didn't care and the benefactor agreed with her. They became friends with each other, including the boy's mother who became a nun. The niece would go to visit her and tell her that grandfather did not want her to marry the doctor. The aunt would reply, «Look for answers in your heart.»

Albertico sends her a bouquet of flowers and the aunt tells the niece that this gesture was very important. One day he wanted to meet the aunt, he told her that he had no last name and the aunt looked at him. He kept going to his grandfather's house and he wanted to meet her house. When he realizes that it was the same black woman who took the child, the man made efforts and talks to her, claiming several things. She tells him: «The grandson that you sent away left the house».

Staggering, he arrives outside and faints. The driver picks him up and takes him home. The wife knew nothing and calls Albertico. He already knew it was his grandson but could not speak. The nun goes to see his father, but it is impossible for his father to speak. She goes to see the house and meets her nanny. She claims that in all these years he never looked for her, but the nanny defends herself, she tells him that he is lying, that she was working and that she had not looked for her either. During this discussion, Albertico enters, realizes that she is his mother and hugs them both.

Albertico marries the rich man's granddaughter. They had a child and they both say that the right to be born cannot be denied.

# 14

# ITALY, LAND OF EMIGRANTS

In 1652, emigration began all over the world. At that time there was no communication, there were only carrier pigeons. There was a coal train, dirt roads and dirt tracks. The water was drawn from the well and it was rainwater. The vegetation was bad, there were no chemicals, there was no industry, only some pasta factory. Commerce had very few products, only what the soil produced.

There were marquises and counts getting rich off the poor. It was the Spaniards who benefited until everyone got tired of living as slaves and revolted. There were the Sicilian Vespers: late in the day men, women and children came out, saying the word *ciciri*. Whoever did not know how to pronounce it correctly was out. At last Sicily was left alone with its people, a marquisate remained and there were great personalities who ruled the towns. The citizens struggled to survive and it was the world of the unequal.

The religion was of Christ, Catholic. All the priests came from Cefalù and the women wore mantillas. The feast of the virgins was celebrated in all the towns and there was the church of Jesus that was built by the princess Lucrezia Millaccio in the XVII century. There was confraternity and there was a Calvary in all the villages, a cemetery where the dead were thrown without anything from above. There were many abbots and there are too many to name.

There were illustrious people and great academies in Palermo:

- Dr. Giuseppe Millaccio

- Ignacio Valturo, sentenced to death

- Priest Doctor Andrea Pascuale, a great theologian

- Monsignor Mercurio Maria Teresa

- Abbé Cipolla, the King's confidant

- Bishop López

- Dr. Gaetano Salemi

- Monsignor Andrea, Napoleon's army doctor

- Ferdinand III

- Abbé Ignacio Salemi.

- Archpriest Sicata

- Abbé Moscarella, farewell to Venice and judge conclave

- Father Cipolla, Capuchin preacher

- Professor Eugenio Salamine, stood out with his personality.

- Father Alfonso, was Turkish

- General Cipolla, you had a lot of love for your country

- Dr. Marchesano, your career in medicine

- Monsignor Saeli, who went to Naples and Rome to teach others, was a born poet.

- the tomb of Doctor Siragusa.

There are also many very painful memories, such as cholera in Sicily. In India and China that dangerous disease started. Father Clares made a promise to be the last to die. The cholera disappeared and returned in 1867, but it did not last long.

15

# BATTLE OF THE VOLTURNO RIVER

In the battle of August 20, 1860, the martyrs remained. After the fall of Napoleon, Italy was divided into small states and fell into misery. The homeland of Dante, Columbus, Galileo, Raffaello, Bellini, all illustrious men. The heroes of Italian independence, the sons of Italy, dead, poor and miserable. Palermo was under the worst Bourbon government and could not have freedom.

King Vittorio Emanuele II, the greatest of the time, saw all that battle. Martin Gaeta, costly Rome. Pius IX, the judgment given to him in Europe where all the newspapers congratulated him. Garibaldi, strong man of France, his existence wins all the wars. Father Giovanangelo, martyr of the Ganea.

They made a committee with the dictator Giuseppe Garibaldi, commander and general chief, national strongman in Sicily. During the reign of Vittorio Emanuele II, Italy had many revolts, especially in Sicily. Revolutionary is the people going hungry. On August 5 the citizens fought with the bourgeois for land and several were shot. Garibaldi sent on their behalf an official of the rich families.

The glorious police on August 20, 1860, had much hatred with improvised politicians. The noble people of Sicily survive the misery. The priest Calogero is Magio Di Giovanni. The owners were given land, melons and wine. They cancelled the pact with a blood God.

On the day of the blood, all was quiet and with the threat of death. A fatal day. Where are all these people going? It is destruction from every side. If you see death, it's Satan, Oh creator, lay your hands!

Nero saw in Rome what happened. The victims were the priest Stefanino il Calabrese, Giovanni Magio, the priest Gaetano Battalla, Giuseppe Saleme, architect Filippo, Vincenzo Saleme, Andres Cutrona, Antonino Girafisi, Angelo Graziano. All were in agony and Father Giovanni Magio is badly wounded. The granddaughter kisses him and runs. Giovanni looked at the assassins and they shot him.

The honorable Cicero and the priest Gaetano Battalla were shot. Father Battalla was of the congregation of Mary SS. of Carmel and in the archive is Gaetano Battalla, the excellent of the Immaculate Conception, president of the confraternity of Mount Carmel, confessional and ordinary. Onofrio Sapienza, stabbed. Giuseppe Saleme was killed (1854-79). Morriales, Benedetti, Nescu, Salemi.

Peppi did not know how to defend himself, the first blow was made by the NN and then by Catalano. Mr. Salemi is armed with blood. Archpriest G. Licato, Brother Filippo, Archpriest Calogero Licata. Mother Church prayed for all. Reverend Licata and the sacristan were all unhappy, that was their affair.

Biagio Valvo, on that bloody day with Meri, hated the minister of God. He looks at the murderers, lies down on the straw and says: «My God, how happy I am in this bed». The brother tells him that he must have courage, for this will not last forever.

Vincenzo Salemi, another criminal, walks away from the bloody campaign. His wife grabs their children and hugs them; she is afraid, abandons the family and runs to save her children. They go to the river where no one sees them. The husband approaches the scaffold, eyes in the air. He does not know how to save himself from death, his heart is pounding, everyone has left him in mortal pain, he is feverish and cold. Vincenzo is tired and leans his head against the tree, where he entrusts himself to fate. An assassin comes to meet him. He shouts: «Save my life, Mary Immaculate. My brother, save my daughter, my wife and my mother. Save me.»

He falls to the ground and does not know what killed him.

Andrea Cutrona and Antonino Girafisi. Andrea Cutrona goes to the field so as not to find them, follows him and kills them. He puts Dioguardi, Sciolino, Riili, Licata and Panzarella in the hole. They seek to destroy families, all is lost, but the eyes of God do not leave. Suddenly the head of Captain Stefano

Scuasa sees the poor of the militia. They marched in the dying village, the Peratolo. They put them on the walls of Father Gialombardo, in the house of Gilantomor.

Why this patriotic martyrdom? Like Christian martyrdom, it is the greatest. Long live Italy! Help the brothers, for they were all honest. From despair to hope, the council of war meets and the rioters are condemned to death in a trial.

The sentence, in the name of Vittorio Emanuele, King of Italy, July 21, 1800. With Messrs. Stefano Scuasa, Captain commander of the mobile colony; Agustino Quatroochi; Captain Lucio D'assaro; Lieutenant Giuseppe Palmesano; Sergeant Major Biagio Raimundo Caporale. With the intervention of the lieutenant, Mr. Rosario Balsamo, authorized prosecuting attorney, with the assistance of the lieutenant Mr. Girolamo Eunice, authorizes the chancellor to search for the named: Giolino Valenti, Filippo Gerace, Leonardo Gialombardo, Maestro Antonio Parisi, Giuseppe Gullo, Giovanni Patti, Biagio Gioia, Carmelo Lombardo.

All from Sicily, Montemaggiore Belsito, accused of swindling and being thugs of the priest Stefano Maggio, Giovanni Maggio, Gaetano Battalla and Antonino Girafisi.

16

# JULIETTA AND ROMEO NOVEL: CHILDREN OF DELINQUENTS

This happened in Alia's village. There was a rich gentleman and his cousin who loved Julietta, but she didn't love him. Her mother told her he was a good match and she said, «I don't love Gaetano.»

One day Julietta falls ill and with a bunch of violets in her hands, she gives Romeo her last look, her last breath and dies. Romeo is left in despair on the last Sunday of Carnival, with the beauty Julietta. With his head resting on a pier, Romeo was very sad, his eyes fixed on the floor, his breath coming from his soul. He wondered why love is like this.

With Romeo's name on her lips, the name she repeated every moment. She dreams and gets up from the piano tired, with her eyes on the moon she begins to sing:

«Grave is my heart, peace I want from God. I want to meet him in life and I never can. The grave in front of me is all weeping. The earth is not mine, it is a dismal dementia. The poor head at my window, the sun to see him alone with my roof, with his precious face, with magic power.»

As the soul sweetly looks at him in the window. With much affection, she lifts her heart, puts her hand to her breast with a kiss of death and begins to cry. He revives a little and sings the Ave Maria. She wanted to sing and could not, she abandoned herself on the sofa. He began to play the piano and could not. He contemplates the moon, that merciless of his passion.

His mother is at the door.

«Julietta, why alone, always alone?».

«My mother, I am unhappy. I spend the most beautiful days sad.»

«My daughter, life is only one. You have to follow the routine of life as our parents did, we have lived like the criminals we were and will be until death. You do not abandon yourself. »

Romeo will be here any minute, but he's not going to leave his mother alone for you. She is very sick and can't walk. She lives in a small town, a village you might say, where there is nothing, no food, no water. How can you leave her alone?

In comparison, we live very happily. We have food, water, good clothing. You lack nothing, nothing at all. Even the church is close by, good beaches, good mountains. We have furniture and even a piano and a man who teaches you to play and sing. Your father is a big crook who steals from others to give you a good living. So cheer up Julietta, you will have to marry Gaetano and like us he will give you a good life».

«I love him not, and will marry Romeo. Mother, I need you, come, you must comfort me. I am sad and lonely, I want you to accompany me.»

«Daughter happiness is in you, you don't have to suffer.»

«For some time now I have had ice in my heart, I have no courage from so much feeling. No matter how much love I have, there is no cure for love. Tears bathe my heart and soul. Mother, I am unhappy, I have not seen Romeo for a long time».

The mother tells him:

«At your age life is smiling at you. I don't get the cause of your unhappiness, tell me what you have, why do you suffer?».

«Last year when I was at the beach, my dad told me a lot of stories, he was unfortunate and had his sorrows, but I felt sad at heart. I did not have the strength to love.»

«Lift your spirits and you will be happy, your cousin will give you a good life.»

«I don't want him,» was the reply. «I want Romeo.»

Romeo gives Julietta her first kiss. He turns around because he sees a shadow, but nothing, it was a dog. He goes to the beach and turns back. He sees in the dark a shadow and comes closer, it was Julietta, there waiting for the angel of her comfort. She pronounces a name in the dark: Julietta, Romeo, I love you...

They approach the room. They look for a lamp with oil, a table and sit opposite each other. Her beloved young man was there, looking at her in the dark. Julietta says to him:

«I've carried your image in my heart for a long time. Everything annoys me when I'm not with you. I love you too much.»

«I can't walk away, I'm sad.»

She replies:

«Since that night I haven't seen you.»

«My mother is sick, I had to be by her side and now she is fine.»

«Tell me about her, tell me if she is happy.»

«My mother is not happy, she is not like so many happy ladies. She is always sad and sacrificed to great affection. That is the continuous battle of life. She falls down without strength because of the heat.»

«Your mom, Romeo, deserves the comfort of great pain.»

«This is my dream, to see my mother happy. We are the children of gangsters. Sometimes I see a smile on my mother's mouth, but then she quickly disappears into battle and life goes on. You get used to the comments, but this is life, Julietta. My mother is very good and wants me to be happy, all under one roof, looking out of her bedroom window at her face.»

«Do it for your mother. Her great pains, comfort her.»

«This is my dream, Julietta. Maybe it's your love that pushes me. We have to see the sacrifice of the greatness of a love. My mom is a simple woman, but respectful. Sometimes I burst with hope, but then I see my mother's eyes looking at me with affection. The greater the danger, the more warmth there is in the family, Julietta. I don't want to live far from my mother, she is very good, I don't want to leave my mother with her great pains.»

In the meantime, a sound of very stealthy footsteps is heard. It was the old squire who went to see the horses and then went back to sleep. The presence of that gentleman makes the bride and groom perceptive and they say goodbye. These are carnival days. She leaves him early, shakes his hand, embraces him, their hearts beat. Romeo is on the street and embraces her passionately.

There is a knock at the door. Mazzini's works are on the table when Eugenio, his best friend, enters with a very troubled face.

«What's wrong with you, why are you like this?» says Romeo.

«The telegrams from Africa are a terrible catastrophe, many dead, people sacrificed, the end of the world. The African enterprise is dismal, no one would have seen such a disaster.»

The cradle of science: Ptolemy, Hannibal and Scipio, the city of Menfi, from Carthage to Alexandria. Until in his dream he had the cup of Caesar, a monument as hero and martyr. Italy weeps, Africa does not laugh. Segati, Dogali, Amba Alagi, Machale, Adria. It shows the barbarians who want the blood of Italy: Menelik, Maconen, Mancascio, Res Alula. Savage people confess that they want the blood of Italy and of the sons of Italy.

They carry the genes of the parents and are their descendants. They carry the eagles of Campidoglio and they all fly to the Arctic. They knew how to tame Gauls, Germans, Cimbrians, Scythians and Carthaginians. A strong and powerful people that folded their knees. They went to risk their lives, fighting with all their strength against their enemies. They could not and died. Compassion is vile and leaves much affection in the hearts of the Italians. What will Europe say, agitated by different feelings.

«Eugenio, the Greeks were glorious. Poor Italy, Eugenio. Italy, the cradle of civility and the first in the world, does not deserve it. In recent times with so much war and inequality, the many telegrams coming from Africa. For her to die, she leaves heir of civilizations and loves to the Italians. What does Europe say? That it is the cradle of gold.»

The Greeks were glorious for 300 Spartans who fell at Thermopylae. Italy preserves the dirty memory of the dead of Novara, Ceferina, San Quintino, Custoza. Napoleon says that the Italians who died with weapons in hand towards the pyramids are brave. In Russia assassins, Waterloo, France, several newcomers from Sudan record several pages. Glorious Pompeii, Marius and Sulla, Hannibal and Hamilcar, Themistocles and Aristides.

Courageous in loss and victory was Italy. There are reasons behind so much hard work and great criminals. Instead, Italy has great heroes, soldiers, victims, maimed. They will call as great heroes the victims of the Germans, suffered the happiness of the black African continent and fought for the good of Italy. To die for the fatherland. There is the grave, although the life of immortality, history will tell, the volumes will live in the immortal pages of Cristoforis, Toselli, Galliani, Da Barmida, Arimondi.

Thousands and thousands die with the name of Italy as their last word. «Long live Italy!» Those who were gravely ill died with the name of Italy in their mouths and in their minds.»

«Romeo, when the war is over are you going to Julietta's?»

«I can't live away from my Julietta.»

Julietta writes him a letter that reads:

«I am sad, melancholy and dead at heart. I spend the hours in tears, melancholy, dead inside and without hope. Near the sun I saw you galloping, with hope for me to see you at the door. Galloping on a white horse, so I remember. I also remember a golden cage, with clear lights, cold and darkness. Stars shining, shining stars, all rescue me and take me to the firmament. It's warm, my heart is happy and bad dreams are driven away.

You departed Romeo, you left me alone with my sadness. It comforts my heart remembering your eternal love. The bells are ringing joyfully, a song of angels at your departure. It was serious, even the moon was darkened, When will we meet again? Remember me. My father and mother know our love, how much we love each other. Come quickly my heart. »

Romeo finishes reading, cries tirelessly and says:

«Beautiful creature, it is not a short time that I have been away from her. It still beats in my heart the man. If he takes the wine and makes it does not want to get drunk, love, the nature of fire, a flame is lit, a love that does not leave. My heart on fire that does not go out and begins to respond before personally. Oh, my love, I will read the letter many times, tears advance slowly.»

Julietta tells him:

«I'm going on another trip. Yes, I am a delinquent's daughter and I have to follow my father, through thick and thin. Everything is in God's hands.»

As he was walking away, Romeo lies down and says:

«Julietta, let me have a drop.»

«I leave it to you. We will die together, my love. A kiss of death.»

17

# STORY OF A WOMAN DECEIVED BY AN UNSCRUPULOUS GENTLEMAN

Francesco did his compulsory military service in Trieste, where he met a rich lady and unscrupulously romanced her. She fell in love with the stranger, who was very vain. She told the father and he replied that she did not want to, that she was an only child. She insisted and the father told her: «If you go with that stranger, don't come back.»

Every palace they saw, she would say to him: «Is this the right one?» He would answer no, that it was better, higher and more beautiful. Until she arrived in the village of Alia, a very beautiful village that has plains and mountains, but he took her to an area outside the village, very poor.

When she entered the shack, it was so poor and with a small bed with a straw mattress, a kitchen that was a wood stove, black and dirty. Poor Doña Oiola, she had no way to complain and was left alone with the love of her life.

He never thought her father was going to throw her out of the house, he thought she was going to enjoy the wealth and he was wrong. When her father kicked her out of the house, she took clothes and fancy lady paints. She wore them to cook, wash and go to fill water. But all the people criticized her when she went outside. He would go to the country and leave her alone, arriving dirty and with his shoes full of dirt.

The floor was dirt, a real mess, but all she cared about was the man who loved her and with whom she had fallen in love. There was no turning back. When she went to fill up the water at the time the boys came out of school, they shouted to her: «Lady Oiola with three canola, one dances for you and two ring for you.»

She was getting old and wrinkled, but always in her fancy dress and paint. She never complained. That's the bottom line: a woman truly in love like that. It would be unthinkable that a woman in love would subject herself to so much bad life and need that she could endure for love. Let the youth follow her example, if they are truly in love.

18

# MEN DON'T CRY

man's heart has to bear in silence all the love affairs and negative feelings. The woman does not understand feelings, she knows that she has to live well and does not want to work, or do housework and even less cook. She goes to eat in hamburger and hot dog places, teaches the children to eat that kind of food and they grow up not wanting to do anything. A lot of homelessness.

If you see a dirty boy begging in the street, it is because his parents have a bad upbringing. He takes drugs, which is the worst, or steals. Is it necessary to reach such a deplorable situation? It is necessary to make a parenthesis: All is not lost. There are many very good, hard-working families who teach their children to study and work, and they grow up like gentlemen. They dress very well, spending little, eating well and dressing well. These are good parents, with good education. It is admirable, that is called knowing how to live.

**19**

## WOMAN WITHOUT SHAME

«My love, why do you have your breast and leg out?».

«To look more interesting with men.»

«I don't like it.»

«If you don't like it, leave me, but you keep me.»

«Me, if I leave, I don't come back and I don't support you.»

«You can leave, but you have to support me. If you don't, I'll denounce you. My love, I can get a better match than you, someone who has money, some young man. That it's you, a real young man who's crazy about me. Men fall to their knees when they see a breast out.»

Angel, a friend tells him: «Friend, don't go on with that woman, she's not for you.»

He replies:

«I love her and if she leaves me, I'll kill myself. She is my life».

«You won't leave me until I want you to, you're crazy about me. You should know that I stopped loving you. I'm using you for the money you give me. I have someone else and I'm taking advantage of you. You are crying for me.»

What craziness! In my time there was respect for men. Today it is a disgrace.

**20**

# THE MAFIA OF MY LAND

This is the story of the land where I was born. 200 years ago there was a *mafioso* named Salvatore Piedra. He was a landowner in the capital of my land.

A psychic lady passes by and tells him that she can read his palm. He accepted and she tells him that he will be rich and so will his children, but his grandchildren will crawl like stray dogs on the ground. He replies, «Get out of here. If you don't, I'll threaten you.»

They were in charge of bribing people to force them to give them daily or they would put them in jail, threatening to kill them. That was the Mafia. With his companions, he acted in several countries, bribing, stealing animals and cattle, crops. In the nearby capital, business owners had to pay him vaccine.

They grew rich and robbed people wherever they went. They were so rich that they gave themselves the title of knights. In a very notorious case, there was a great cattle robbery and they managed to put two sons in jail for thirty years. One of the sons of this gentleman had studied to be a lawyer. When he was coming out of the courthouse stairs, he came down and one of the brothers was killed. The other one, after 30 years, came out to speak on the balcony, next to his grandmother and son.

Their names were Fermin, Jorge and Rafael. The grandchildren Martino, Momo, Hector, Agustin, Giuleb, Carlitto, Salvatore. All of them were born happy to be rich, holding in their hands the title of knights. The father thought they would be Mafiosos, but none of them followed him, neither the grandsons nor the sons.

The thugs that loom over the old man will feel lost and will hide for many years. The war began and there was Mussolini, who had finished with the Mafia. For forty years no one will know about them, the family becomes a shadow and no one is seen anymore.

The Mafioso's sons, Fermín, Jorge and Rafael, were very quiet, they didn't know what their father had done with the Mafia. They married rich people and went to the fairs with their impeccable dress. One of the wives, when the husband arrived, would throw away all the clothes.

One round, a child was sick and told the service not to touch the door handle. The child thinks about it and decides not to listen to the mother. He tells her not to listen to her. When the time came and as if she did not know, the woman did not cooperate. They were cut off and they mortgaged the whole property because they did not know how to manage the palace. They sold everything they had made. There were many people buying gold coins, vases, statues and the piano they played.

A lot of people went crazy to spend on sales. None of them thought about it. With rich people and friends, they did not know how to manage. They lost everything, just as the fortune teller had predicted, and then they bought a threshing machine on credit. The neighbors fed them. The wife had no more hope and when friends had birthdays, they did not send them dishes.

Once she went to her father to thresh grain and had her boots tied with wire. The father told her that the girl had a lot of intelligence and asked her to do a two-digit multiplication mentally. Suddenly she did it, at the age of eight.

The oldest grandson, Martino, was studying Agricultural Engineering. They had to have a change, a large agrarian distribution and a socialist Italy, in which there were many agrarian reforms. He married a rich woman, a car manufacturer. He had the title and they were all very nice.

His brother was a high school graduate, but he went back to stealing animals. They stole everything they could find and put innocent people in jail. The others went to the stables, but a few of them went to see their father, who was in serious condition. He had gone to camp and one of them was in the pass.

One of the cousins worked with a travel agency. At that travel agency, KLN, an employee asked him if he was coming to visit Venezuela. He replied: «With what money? I am not an executive, I am an employee who was with the Mafia and met her when they were children.»

21

# HISTORY OF MY TOWN:<br>ALIA 1615-1860

Alia was at that time a fief of the XVII century. Sicily was under Spanish rule thanks to King Filippo III and Pietro Celeste, Baron and Marquis of Santa Croce, a politician of the time on behalf of his wife, Francesca Cifuentes.

Barbara thanks to the colonizations of the country of Alia, the decree of concession in Madrid, May 7, 1615, by the decompensation of the monarch and the feudatory in the following years, 1623. For 200 years the Baron and Marquis remained the owner of Alia. Sicily was divided and Palermo was called «The Golden Conch».

Giovanni Vega. Manzara val Dermone hires Santuzi Chianchitelli. Belatassa Lavatore, Barbara Timpi D'arsala, Marco Tubianco, Cozo de Ciciro, Setepate Vauso, Bacuce Quatroponte, Pass of the Marquis of Santa Rosalia, Valley of the

Innocents, Agualonca Burdine, Bevario Bosco Cozzo, Cuerva Sanguinche.

## 22

# AGAINST THE MAFIA

There were many people who fought against the Mafia. I knew my husband's godfather, who confirmed him and the cousin who married one of them.

He worked against the Mafia and fed the entire prison in Palermo. They benefited by exporting tomatoes and coal to the United States, but this did not last long. Several merchants collaborated with him.

The father left us the entire Arquímedes Street in Palermo. Unfortunately, little by little, it was completely lost. He lived in a small two-room apartment, but unfortunately he was unlucky and was killed by the Mafia.

All those who were against the Mafia, sooner or later end badly. This is the sad story.

**23**

# THE GREAT CRIMINALS
# OF THE WORLD

Lucio Drago was born in Montemaggiore. As a young man, he had been very studious, although in religion. At that time there were many attacks and Vittorio Emanuele III was the King of Italy. There were great criminals, like Gioja and Dolores. So many young people sacrificed for humanity, it was serious at that time. Giuseppe Garibaldi says it was a miscarriage of justice, but there was money through the Mafia.

Among the best known names of the time were the brothers Agostino, Antonino, Rosalino and Vincenzo Drago Salemi. This happened when my father was not yet born. There was a cultural work in favor of Rosalino Liboria and Virginia Rosa Vasallo, the Drago family, who lived next door to my grandmother.

Agostino was killed on the scaffold and Antonino in prison. Rosalino and Vincenzo got out of prison alive after 30 years.

The mother died of a broken heart and a worker of Salvo complicated the family. 30 years... poor mother. Misery and death, Sicily invaded by corruption after the First World War.

Pipitunazo, Passo di Lupo, Tirdinare Sena, his dream was an extension Bravatura and seeks it in the document. In 1296 the throne of Sicily was occupied by Federico H. D'Aragona, by the Barons and Marquises. It was a good possibility of government. The brother Di Giacomo II, King of Aragon, left the power to Charles II, owner of Naples, who rebelled with the brother Boniface VIII and remained in Sicily. He was the originator of the Sicilian Vespers, in which men, women and children took part.

In 1282 Giovanni di Mileto of Palizzo, heir of Mateo, belonged to a family of Catalonian origin. In the fief of Alia another story begins on May 5, 1366, with the act of Giacomo di Starano, from Palermo. The fief of Alia passed into the possession of Reinaldo Crispi and the Castle of San Nicolo was left to his heirs, who were to remain in Sicily under the rule of King Federico and his heir. They sold all that fief and it was verified by King Federico. The heir of Crispi was obliged to the obligatory military service, of horse armed by the owner for 20 ounces of gold of the fief.

Reinaldo Crispi, heir because of the rebellion of King Martino and Queen Maria, returns to the birthplace of the feudatory of Alia. They took the property in 1397, when Guglielmo di Lazaro took possession according to the document of Giacomo Crispi. At the time of Vicari's rule, with large fiefs of Martino, the loss of the fief property was linked to the form of vassalage of Guglielmo Lijano, the last feudal hierarch. There was no strength to win the dispute to Henry, son of Giacomo, who had asserted the region.

On October 10, 1401, King Martino appointed Enrico Crispi as heir. In 1406 and 1414, the captain of justice of Trapani, very prestigious in Alia, advanced financially, as well as the brother Pietro Romano, son Giovanni. In 1461 it passed into the possession of the same family and Crispi sold Alia to Vincenzo Imbarbaria, for the sum of eleven gold.

The right is reserved by my heirs, Vincenzo Imbarbaria with Eleonora Crispi of Federico, with union of Baron Pietro and three women: Laura Pallisera Tortorice. After the death of the husband, Eleonora is left with the little Pietro, heir, as well as the accounts and the slaves, on May 7, 1537.

The undersigned domiciled in Montemaggiore Belsito, Andres Drago Saleme, went directly to the delegation P. S. and is in Montemaggiore, coming from the court of Termine Merese. The Cardinal was Calogero and consummate eyewitness. He knows the P. S. Alessandra Concetta, wife of Giuseppe Battaglia, domiciled in Alia.

Meet the real killer, Gualcuno Pagano with a black beard and Ponazo Privera with a white beard. They all transformed with painted beards and hid with the money stolen from the murderer Di Marco. Panepinto Anna, Antonino Panepinto, Rosalia. It was the nuncio, who knows the grave circumstances. Solito Giochino and the wife of Cotone Nicolo.

These are the real culprits, murderers, who have lost her husband and caused a conflict with the police. She is in America and enjoys the bacchanals with dollars they stole from Di Marco, Battalla and Concetta, in Alia. He could not hide the crime and declares that he was Cotone's son and dies in the distant land of America.

Mr. Bernardo Mulé Si Stefano returned to Alia. Cotone, Cuponazo, Pagano and Solito were charged and justice triumphed. Agostino Drago was executed with his great condemnation, while Antonio died of heartbreak. Drago, Rosolino, Vincenzo, Di Salvo, Francesco il Cugino, in the penal bath of Procida and Ancola.

The undersigned, grandson of the innocent man, places himself at the disposal of the E. V. to know the truth. The family and the state stole, regardless of the law or conscience. The Drago family did not own any property. They are related to senators, deputies and lawyers for knowing the truth. E. V. III that justice is expected so much subscribes I E. V. A review is ordered and to be done by magistrates outside the community of Alia. Resident of Montemaggiore Belsito, October 5, 1901.

Andrea Drago Salemi denounces the procurator, representative of the trial at the court of Termine Merese. Cardinal Lucio was Calogero, eyewitness where it is known in Alia about gifts to Rosalia Di Marco. The court was corrupt in a small village, Alia. What will it be in all Sicily?

On the night of July 31 and August 1, 1872, thieves and bad people came out. A poor old lady in her eighties called majata. The poor old lady lived with her grandson Di Marco and they made her disappear. They brought the corpse close to the bed and put it in the fire. The neighbors alerted and watched the fire until the relatives and the authorities arrived.

None of the neighbors spoke, because they were afraid. Two infamous people called Brother Drago's name and the authorities arrested him. They had found a chicken on the table, with the cutlery, because he was waiting for his grandson to eat. He had come from Montemaggiore and was returning that day. While he was arriving, the authorities exchanged the chicken's blood for human blood. Big mistake! The boy was not in the village, he was working the land and the cows.

Di Marco's grandson found her in agony and was told that those who had been there had not been able to speak because of the gravity, that she had a hole in her throat with a lot of pain. They were asking who he was and since he could not speak, it was enough to condemn him at the Assisi Court of Palermo. The brothers were sent to jail. One of the brothers tells the court that the blood was from the chicken, but they insist that it was human blood.

Di Marco was taken to the Court of Assisi, Palermo, on August 29, 1873. On May 12 was Agostino and was executed in 1874 in the prison of Palermo, with dead eyes and tired of crying. He was preparing to go to the scaffold in the small cell illuminated with a funeral lamp. He sees an image on the wall and says with his eyes to heaven: «My God, have mercy on me, I am innocent,» thinking of his mother. «I am innocent.»

He closes his eyes and opens them thinking of his poor mother. The Augustinian Drago priest arrives, the time has come and they were waiting for him. He tells him: «The time has come.» He gives him the crucifix to kiss and goes to the gallows. First he speaks and says «Aliesi, I am innocent. They have taken me to the gallows, but I am innocent.» He kisses the crucifix. Everything happens and he is dead, decapitated. The father says: «I must pray for this sinner, they don't know what they have done.»

It was a sunny day in Palermo. To the Palermitans who had attended the event, Father gives them a souvenir: «Brothers, people of Palermo, I invite you to come to St. Lucy's parish to pray for this innocent man.»

Thirty years later, everything was over for the Drago family, as planned. The grandchildren went to look for him. They were Damiano's children and grandchildren. The judges and men of the competent authority, the procurator of Palermo, on the night of July 31 and August 1, 1872, with the procurator of Termine da Cotone, Nicola Pagano, Giovanni Solito, Giochino il Porrazo, Vincenzo, the Cugino of Termine and others from Alia.

Rosalia Di Marco is left in jail with cash. Across the street lived Sabino Di Marco, another mafioso invited by the aunt. The boy Cosimo opens the door and enters to look, dressed as a gangster. He closes the door and wanted to see where the money was. Poor Cosimo dies.

Andrea Drago Salemi in this complaint, the prosecutor rebukes the trial at the court of Termine Merese, Cardinal Lucio was Judge Calogero, eyewitness testimony. It is known of the common eyes of Porrazo, Vincenzo. A Catalonian aunt, Rosa, widow of Battle of Alia, knows the crime for being a confidant of Nero Catalano. The grandson Di Marco goes to see the macifondo, friend of Salvatore.

It was Antonio to destroy the statement in Alia. The unhappy Di Salvo Francesco has seen the court of Assisi incriminated and counting the delegate Rasmondini Vincenzo, in the service of P. S. Termine Merese. He remained in Alia for a long time, S. V. III, 1011. Miceli Salvatore receives the crime of author and Ponazo Vincenzo, Solito Giochino, sends him 1100 with money.

It is indispensable without a lawyer. Salvatore Guccione of Montemaggiore, vice-pretor of Alia at the time of the crime, begins a challenge to the process in 1872. The delegate Gafa, resident of Alia, wants to know the truth at any cost and unravels the truth of the family E. V. III. Justice is expected and therefore, I E. V. reviews in earnest.

# ABOUT THE AUTHOR

Teresa Di Sclafani De Nasca was born in Italy. She has also lived in Venezuela and the United States.

# MORE WORKS BY TERESA
# DI SCLAFANI DE NASCA

- *The world according to Teresa Di Sclafani*

- *The Diary of Teresa Di Sclafani*

- *The Mafia according to Teresa Di Sclafani*

Each title is available in Castilian (aka «Spanish»), English and Italian.